THE Lucky HAT

BY Matthew Henry Hall

ILLUSTRATIONS BY Jim Madsen

Grand Canyon Association

Many years ago, a little boy named Michael lived happily with his Grandma Feather, who kept him safe and fed and warm. Whenever she could, Grandma Feather made Michael little presents—stuffed animals from soft pieces of cloth, cookies covered in powdered sugar, and once a toy train carved out of wood. One winter, she took thread and fabric and love, then stitched them all together to make Michael a *very* special hat.

"Thank you, Grandma," Michael said. With his finger, he traced the letters sewn across the hat's front. "Lucky," he said, smiling. "It says, Lucky."

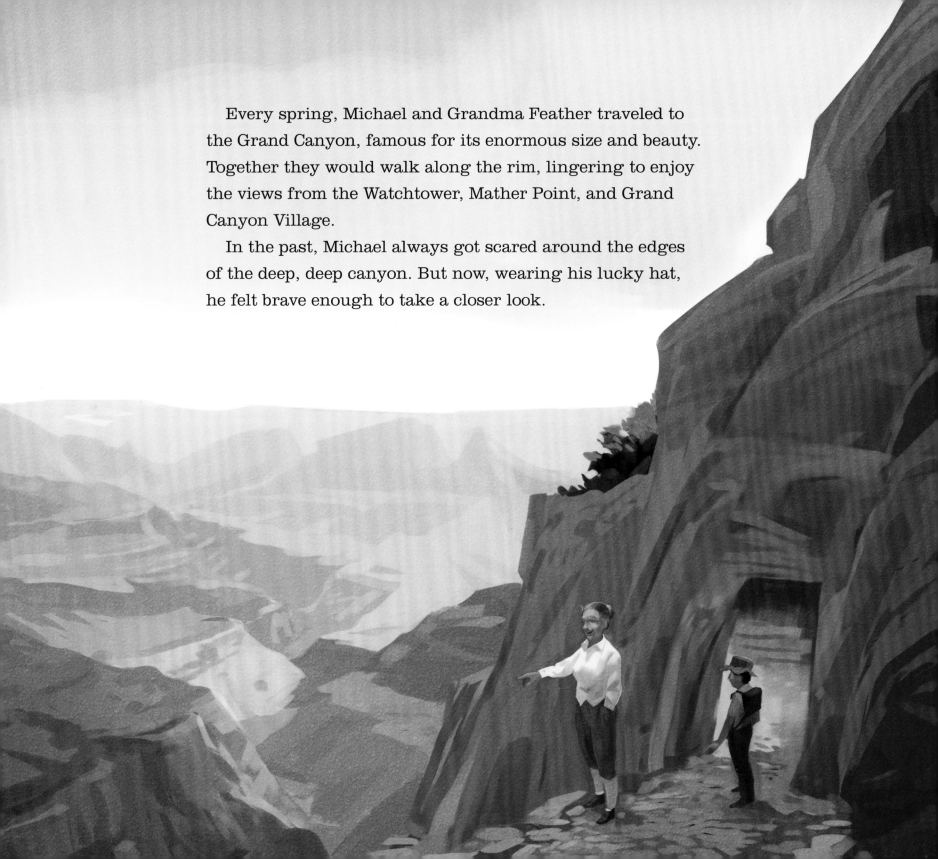

Every spring, Michael and Grandma Feather traveled to
the Grand Canyon, famous for its enormous size and beauty.
Together they would walk along the rim, lingering to enjoy
the views from the Watchtower, Mather Point, and Grand
Canyon Village.

In the past, Michael always got scared around the edges
of the deep, deep canyon. But now, wearing his lucky hat,
he felt brave enough to take a closer look.

"Do people really hike to the bottom?" Michael asked.

"Oh, yes," said Grandma Feather.

Michael tried to imagine himself hiking all the way down to the bottom of the gigantic canyon. *Maybe*, he thought, *I could do it if I was older and if I was wearing my lucky hat.*

But as Michael got older, the hat no longer fit his head.

"Don't worry," said Grandma Feather. Adding a piece of fabric here and a piece of fabric there, she made the hat fit perfectly again.

As the years went by, Grandma Feather restitched the hat over and over, making it a little bigger each time.

When Michael became a teenager, Grandma Feather fixed his hat once more.

"Thank you, Grandma," Michael said, trying it on. "I'm going to hike into the canyon, and now I can wear my lucky hat."

The very next week, Michael hiked deep into the canyon. At mid-day, he rested on a rocky ledge and looked out at the river far below. Michael thought, *I've never felt luckier in all my life.*

Then without warning, the wind rushed in with a roar and snatched up the lucky hat.

"**Noooo!**" yelled Michael.

But the hat flew high above him. Then sailing behind a massive wall of rock, it vanished.

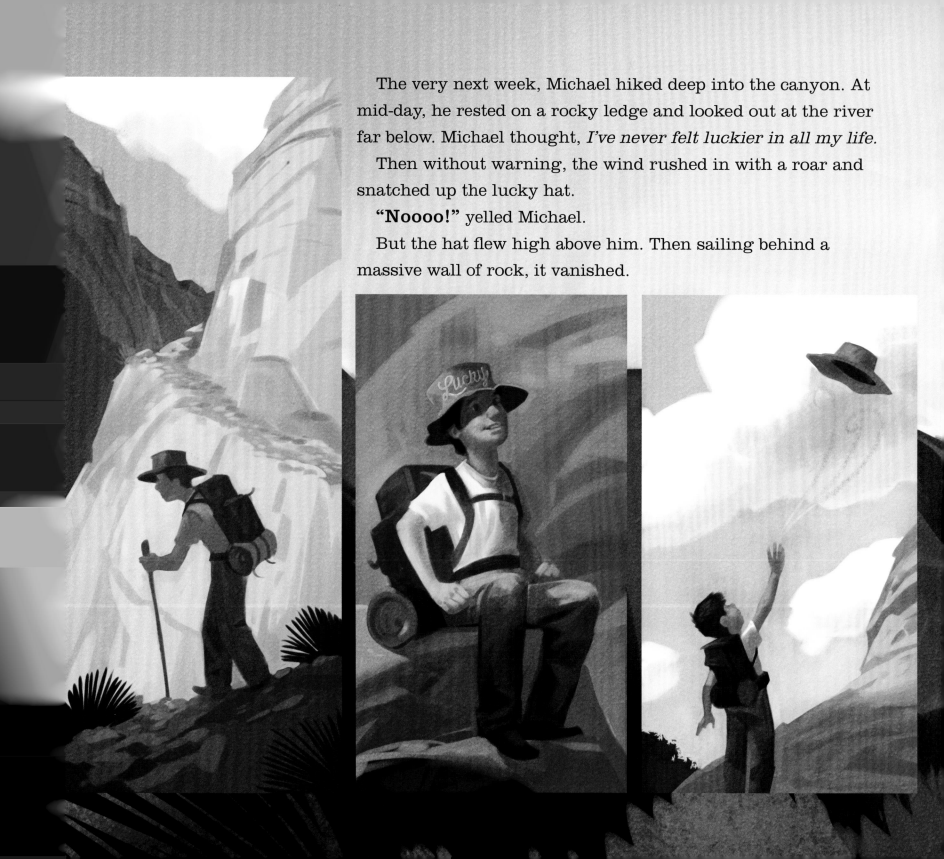

When Michael told Grandma Feather what had happened, she said quietly, "When we lose something we cherish, we often find something else we cherish more."

But Michael was not so sure. Year after year, he returned to the canyon to walk its winding trails and to look for his lucky hat.

One day, Michael met another hiker named Luci. When Michael told Luci about his hat, she went out with him every day to look for it. They did not find the hat, but instead found a very special friendship.

Years later, on Michael and Luci's wedding day, Michael said to Luci, "I've never felt luckier in all my life."

Before long, Michael and Luci had a daughter, Petra, and every year, the whole family hiked at the canyon and looked for Michael's lucky hat.

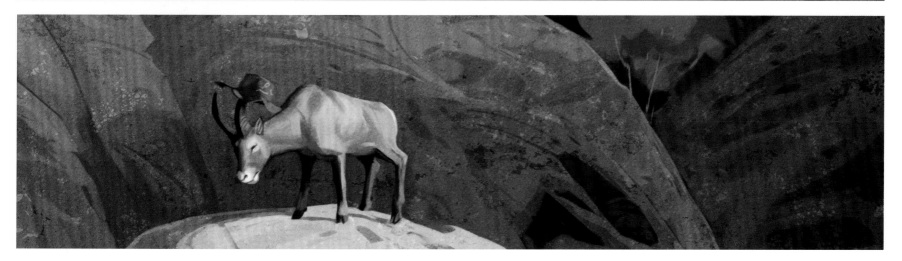

They never found the hat, but they found many other wonderful things—treefrogs and lizards, gurgling creeks and cool pools of water. But the best thing they found was a great joy in being together in such a beautiful place.

One memorable spring, as Michael and his family hiked into the canyon, Michael thought of Grandma Feather and smiled. "Maybe *this* year," he said, "we'll find my lucky hat."

That afternoon, he and Petra went searching for the hat. They looked among the tangled roots of old mesquite trees and in the shadows of huddled giant boulders. They found coral pink prickly pear blossoms and drawings made by people long ago. But they did not find the hat.

"Poppa?" asked Petra. "What made your hat so lucky?"

Michael paused, then said, "Your *Great*-Grandma Feather made that hat. And when I wore it, I always felt safe because I knew how much she loved me."

That night, Petra lay awake, wishing with all her heart she could find her father's lucky hat. Grabbing her flashlight, she snuck out of the tent. Mice scurried away from her flashlight's beam. "Little mice," she whispered. "Have you seen Poppa's lucky hat?"

One mouse stopped, stood up on his hind legs as if he understood, then ran in one determined direction. Petra followed, not noticing the first fine drops of rain.

The mouse came to a halt under an enormous ledge of rock, looked up at Petra, and darted into a tiny hole. Petra peeked into the hole where the mouse disappeared but did not see the hat.

KRAAASSH!! KAAA-BOOOOM!!

Petra whipped around as lightning flashed and crashed, and the canyon echoed with giant booms of thunder.

The rain came down so hard and so fast, Petra could not see the way back to their campsite. Shivering and rocking, she waited for the rain to stop.

Finally, Petra fell into a restless sleep. In a dream, the mouse brought her the lucky hat.

"Here it is!" he said, placing the shimmering hat on her head.

Instantly, she felt safe and warm and loved.

When Petra awoke, the sky was blue. The sun shone brightly, and she heard her father calling her name. "Petra!"

"Poppa!" she answered.

She saw both of her parents running towards her. First, Michael scooped Petra up in a gigantic bear hug, then Luci held her close. In that moment, Petra *knew* she was safe and warm and loved.

Suddenly, she remembered her dream. "Poppa, I think your lucky hat is somewhere near here. We should look for it."

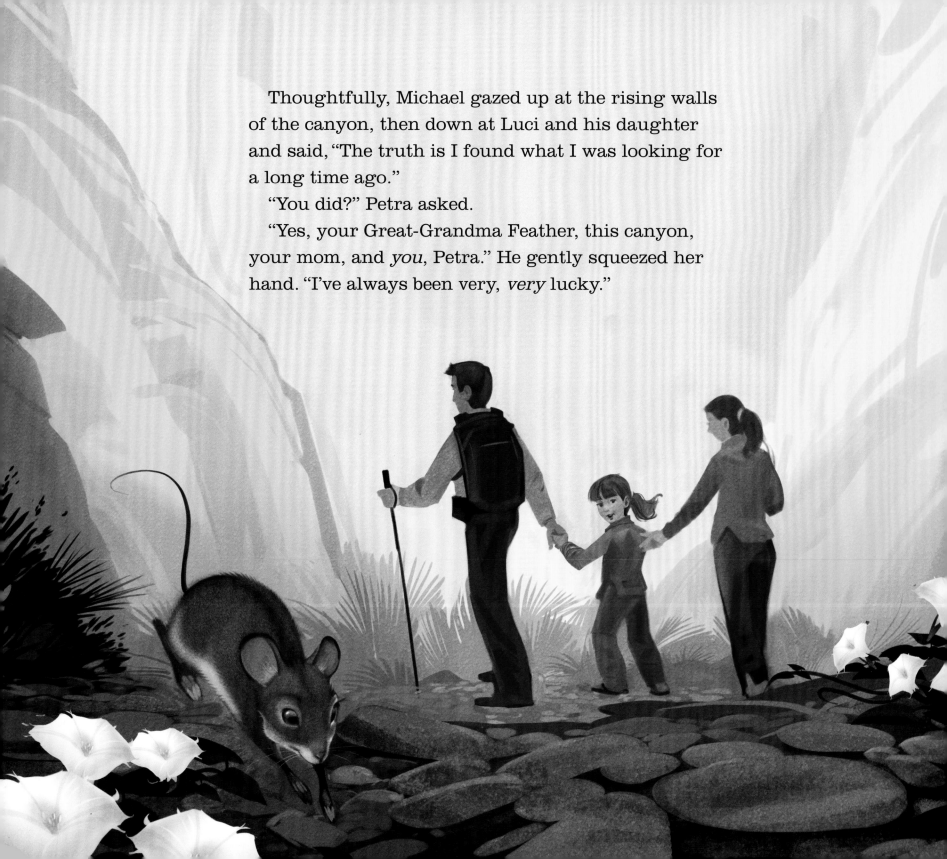

Thoughtfully, Michael gazed up at the rising walls of the canyon, then down at Luci and his daughter and said, "The truth is I found what I was looking for a long time ago."

"You did?" Petra asked.

"Yes, your Great-Grandma Feather, this canyon, your mom, and *you*, Petra." He gently squeezed her hand. "I've always been very, *very* lucky."

North Rim

COMMON
RAVEN

The Hat's Journey

Where did the
Lucky Hat go?

Did you see where the hat went after it flew
off Michael's head? With this map, follow the
hat's journey as it travels by air and land, by
feather, paw, and hoof through Grand Canyon
National Park. How many places and animals
do you recognize?

Where do you think
the hat will go to next?

*(Turn the page
to find out.)*

CANYON
TREEFROG

DEER
MOUSE

Plateau
Point

To
Phantom
Ranch and
Colorado
River

South
Rim

MOUNTAIN
LION

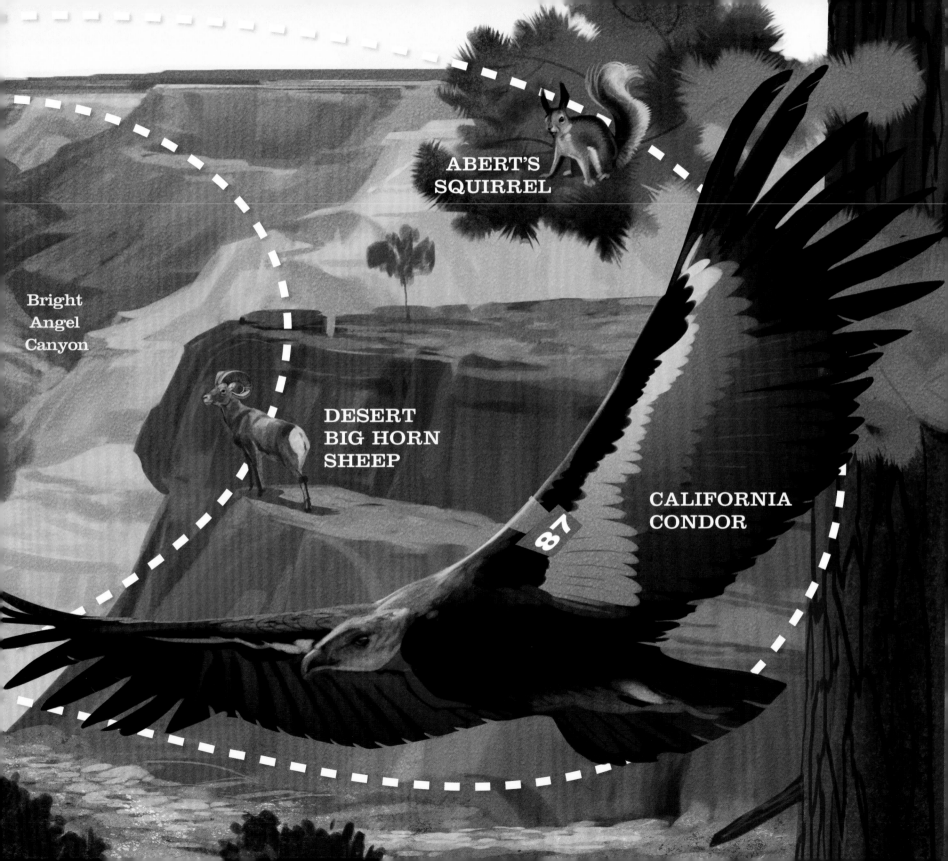

ABERT'S
SQUIRREL

Bright
Angel
Canyon

DESERT
BIG HORN
SHEEP

CALIFORNIA
CONDOR

87